Level 3 is ideal f̶ ̶̶ ̶̶ ̶̶ re developing
reading confidence ̶
to read longer storie̶

Special featur ̶d

Wider
vocabulary,
reinforced
through
repetition

One day, Mother Wolf
heard a roar in the jungle.
It was a tiger called
Shere Khan. He had found a
man-cub and was chasing him.

Longer
sentences

Simple story
structure

"We will keep that man-cub safe,"
Mother Wolf told Father Wolf.
"We will call him Mowgli."

Shere Khan was angry.
He wanted to eat the man-cub.

"I'll be back for him," he roared.

Educational Consultant: Geraldine Taylor
Book Banding Consultant: Kate Ruttle

A catalogue record for this book is available from the British Library

Published by Ladybird Books Ltd
80 Strand, London, WC2R 0RL
A Penguin Company

010
© LADYBIRD BOOKS LTD MMXIV
Ladybird, Read It Yourself and the Ladybird Logo are registered or
unregistered trademarks of Ladybird Books Limited.

ISBN: 978-0-72328-080-4

Printed in China

The Jungle Book

Written by Jillian Powell
Illustrated by Gavin Scott

One day, Mother Wolf
heard a roar in the jungle.

It was a tiger called
Shere Khan. He had found a
man-cub and was chasing him.

"We will keep that man-cub safe,"
Mother Wolf told Father Wolf.
"We will call him Mowgli."

Shere Khan was angry.
He wanted to eat the man-cub.

"I'll be back for him," he roared.

As time went by, Baloo the bear showed Mowgli how to make jungle calls.

Bagheera the panther heard about Mowgli and came to see him.

Mowgli wanted to play
with the monkeys.

But Baloo and Bagheera said,
"You can't trust monkeys. It's not
safe to play with them."

One day, when the bear and the panther were asleep, two monkeys took Mowgli away. He was afraid!

14

Mowgli looked up and saw Chil, the kite. He made a kite call to him and Chil came over.

"Get Baloo and Bagheera to help me!" Mowgli said.

Chil found Baloo and Bagheera, and told them that the monkeys had got Mowgli.

Bagheera said, "Kaa the python will help us. The monkeys are afraid of him."

The monkeys kept Mowgli
in a snake house. He made
a snake call to stop the
snakes biting him.

Then he saw Bagheera the panther! The monkeys jumped on Bagheera and bit him.
"Go in the water!" Mowgli called. "That will stop them."

When Baloo came to help, the monkeys jumped on him, too!

Just then, they heard Kaa the python hiss and the monkeys ran away!

25

Baloo helped Mowgli get
out of the snake house.
Mowgli was safe with
Baloo and Bagheera again.

Some time went by. One day
Bagheera the panther said,
"The wolves want a new leader
and they will not want a man-cub
with them. You are not one
of them, you are not a wolf."

"You are not safe here," said
Bagheera. "Go and live
in the village."

"One day I will come back with
the skin of Shere Khan!" Mowgli
said. "Then the wolves will see
what I can do!"

31

Mowgli went to the village
and all the people came
out to see him. A woman
called Messua said she
was Mowgli's mother.
She looked after him.

33

In the village, Mowgli lived with the people and looked after the buffalo herd.

35

One day when Mowgli was with the buffalo, two wolves came to see him. One of the wolves was called Grey Brother.

"Shere Khan is back. He wants to eat you," said Grey Brother.

"Take half the buffalo herd this way and half that way," said Mowgli.

37

When the tiger came, Mowgli
called the herd.

The buffalo ran right over
Shere Khan!

Mowgli came back with the tiger skin.

The village people said, "We want that skin to sell it."

Mowgli said it was his. The people were very angry.

"You have to go," Messua said. "You are not safe here."

So Mowgli went back to the jungle.

When the wolves saw Shere Khan's skin, they said, "You can be our new leader!"

But Mowgli said, "No, you did not want me with you, so I will live alone."

43

"Trust me," said Grey Brother.
"Live with me."

Mowgli did trust Grey Brother,
so he went to live with him
in the jungle.

And Baloo and Bagheera
were happy that he was safe.

How much do you remember about the story of The Jungle Book? Answer these questions and find out!

- Who is chasing Mowgli in the jungle?

- Who teaches Mowgli to make jungle calls?

- Where do the monkeys take Mowgli?

- Which animals run over Shere Khan?

- Who does Mowgli go to live with at the end?